A ROOKIE READER

RAIN! RAIN!

By Carol Greene

Illustrations by Larry Frederick

Prepared under the direction of Robert Hillerich, Ph.D.

SCHOLASTIC INC.

New York   Toronto   London   Auckland   Sydney
Mexico City   New Delhi   Hong Kong   Buenos Aires

This book is for Becky.

Copyright © 1982 by Regensteiner Publishing Enterprises, Inc.
All rights reserved. Published by Scholastic Inc.,
557 Broadway, New York, NY 10012.
Printed in China.

ISBN 0-516-24545-7

SCHOLASTIC, ROOKIE READER, and associated logos and designs are trademarks and/or
registered trademarks of Scholastic Inc.

7 8 9 10   62   11 10

Rain? Rain?

Will it?

Will it rain?

One cloud.

Two clouds.

8

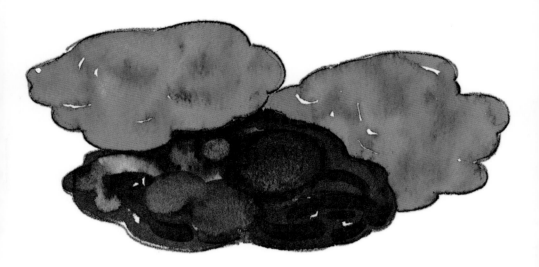

Black clouds.

Blue clouds.

Lightning pop.

Thunder drum.

Rain! Rain!

See it come.

Rain on trees.

Rain on bees.

Rain on trucks.

Rain on ducks.

Rain on towns.

Rain on clowns.

Rain on roof.

Plop. Plop.

Rain on window.

Drop. Drop.

Rain on me.

Rain on you.

Come, see!

Rain in…

PUDDLES!

WORD LIST

		rain
	ducks	roof
bees	in	see
black	it	thunder
blue	lightning	towns
cloud	me	trees
clouds	on	trucks
clowns	one	two
come	plop	will
drop	pop	window
drum	puddles	you

About the Author

Carol Greene has written over 20 books for children, plus stories, poems, songs, and filmstrips. She has also worked as a children's editor and a teacher of writing for children. She received a B.A. in English Literature from Park College, Parkville, Missouri, and an M.A. in Musicology from Indiana University. Ms. Greene lives in St. Louis, Missouri. When she isn't writing, she likes to read, travel, sing, do volunteer work at her church — and write some more. Her *The Super Snoops and the Missing Sleepers* and *Sandra Day O'Connor, First Woman on the Supreme Court* have also been published by Childrens Press.

About the Artist

Larry Frederick is a native of Chicago who now works as a free-lance illustrator in Evanston, Illinois. He studied at the art center school in Los Angeles, California as well as several art schools in the Chicago area. He began his career in advertising art, but for the past fourteen years has worked mainly in book illustration.